A Wayward Oath

Bill Jacques

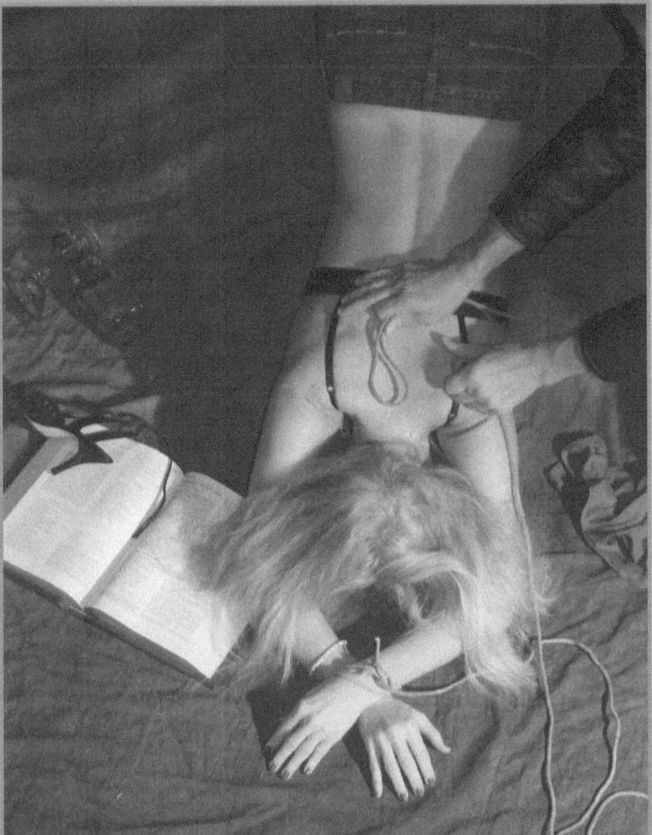

Other books published by

Sweet Dreams Publishing of Massachusetts

Chicken Fried Steak, Action-Adventure
  by Steven I. Dahl, MD

Streets of Rage, A novella
  by Richard Chandler, Writer/Film Director

Ooodle Van Boodle and His Magical Cakes,
A children's story
  by Kim Shanley-Peretti, Olivia and Luke's Mom

Visit us at:
www.PublishAtSweetDreams.com
or
Contact us at:
info@PublishAtSweetDreams.com

"A cold, dark tale of Boston's cold, dark winter. Jacques does an excellent job of capturing the black heart of the city."

Richard Chandler,
Writer/Director of *Heaven and Hell*

"Jacques stages a quick ride through a unique and complex story, using lots of details to bring us into the dark world of Detective Edwards. The sharp and witty detective seems to outsmart even the reader, only revealing his knowledge as needed, until in the end, we're right along with him, as he finds himself involved in a sacrificial ritual, even he may not escape. And along the way we find ourselves in one heck of a story."

Shelly Lanciani,
Writer/Director of *Polly and the Murderers*

"A Wayward Oath is a dark, gritty, fast-paced story that kept me entranced and wanting more. Jacques creates a world that frightened and intrigued me all the way through."

Andrew Bard,
Writer/Director of *Thou Shall Kill*

The Wayward Oath
Cover & Interior Design: Lisa Akoury-Ross
Cover Photos (Front and Back): Michelle Ennis
Published by Sweet Dreams Publishing of Massachusetts
5 Federal Street
Weymouth, MA 02188

For more information about this book contact Lisa Akoury-Ross
at Sweet Dreams Publishing by email at
lross@publishatsweetdreams.com

Library of Congress Control Number: 2010920321

ISBN-10: 0-9824461-2-8
ISBN-13: 978-09824461-2-6

Printed in the United States of America

This book is dedicated to
Chucky and Dottie—
May the love affair never end. . . .

Author's Note

Writing a novel is a solitary, sometimes lonely, act. Finishing a novel and having it published is not. As the old saying goes, "It takes a village," . . . and I have been lucky enough to have some great "townspeople" in my corner.

I want to thank my wife Cheryl for putting up with this time consuming little hobby of mine and for supporting this project from start to finish.

I want to thank my Mom, Anne, for always leaving books lying around for me to read and for her unwavering support in any endeavor I have chosen to take on.

I want to thank my wonderful editors, Jayne Pupek and Patty Moore for taking the time to turn this twisted tale into a readable piece of literature.

I want to thank Michelle Ennis for her awesome cover photography and keen eye for detail. I want to thank Mike Ennis for his direction in "staging" the cover model and Rick Hulbert for the use of his studio.

I also want to thank our lovely model who—in light of this mystery—shall remain nameless until the end of time.

I want to thank Edgar Allen Poe and Shirley Jackson for creating and introducing me to such beautiful and horrific stories as *The Tell Tale Heart* and *The Lottery* when I was just a high school kid with a passion for literature. And that goes double for Stephen King and *Salem's Lot*.

I want to thank writer/director Trevor Wright for simply listening to my description of the story and for believing in its possibility to become a great film someday.

I want to thank my publisher and friend Lisa Akoury-Ross for rescuing *The Wayward Oath* from the scrap heap in my office and for the push to get it into its final incarnation.

I want to thank my two boys, Nolan and Joshua, for their patience, love, and for the smile they put on my face anytime either of them walks into a room.

And I want to thank you, the reader, for choosing to take a break from your busy life to spend an hour or so with a lunatic doctor, a smart-assed detective and a whole lot of strange and mysterious doings.
I hope you enjoyed our time together. Because with you, the reader, in the final mix, the "village" is complete.

Bill Jacques
January 5, 2010

Evil isn't born of Man. . . .
Man is born of Evil. . . .

✧✧✧

The call came in at 3:32 A.M., waking me from the dead of sleep. A call that would change my way of looking at things for a long time to come.

I had been dreaming of someplace warm and tropical; sitting on a lounge chair with a red-colored drink in one hand and a paperback novel in the other. The bright sun was baking my exposed skin, and I couldn't have felt more at ease. The waves lapping the ocean's edge were lulling me into a pleasant trance. The sand at my feet was warm and giving between my toes. A tepid breeze brushed my pores and massaged my temples. At this perfect moment no job related stress existed. No pimps with their greased up-street-smooth tongues swore at me. No loud, smoky booking rooms suffocated me. No hookers reeking of cheap perfume and cheaper smelling back lot sex-rooms propositioning me.

Now there was only peace. Self-gratifying, self-absorbing peace . . .

In the dream, a woman was watching me from her own lounge chair nearby. She was tanned and young and very, very lovely. Her brown hair was pulled back in a pony tail, exposing high cheek-bones bronzed from the sun. Her green and white bikini bathing suit was cut low on the top and nar-row in the hips. She had the longest, smoothest looking legs I had ever seen. I motioned to her and she nodded. She smiled-a perfect white-toothed smile. I smiled back. She paused a moment, seeming to think about something, and suddenly started to rise from her chair in a fluid movement that seemed to take forever, unfolding herself like some wild and exotic animal on the plains of a far away African country. She stood, hesitating slightly again, then headed my way in a manner that could only be described as stately: one sculptured leg passing in front of the other. A slow motion effect that momentarily stopped my heart from beating and my lungs from breathing.

She walked closer still, causing the molecules around us to expand, sending pulses of heatwaves from her body onto mine. I could feel the pound-ing in my ears, sense the blood of my vessel stir-ring in my veins. Her perfect brown body was only a few feet away now and I reached out my right hand towards her. I felt the heat charge from her body mixing with the bright sun. I could smell the lotion on her glazed skin and see the rivulets of perspiration on her upper lip. I noticed that her belly was pierced with a diamond stud and she wore many rings on her fingers. The ocean behind us pounded. We were inches apart. My breath got heavier, my heart beat louder in my chest, the heat in my belly matched by the heat of her gaze. Her lips parted; a slight lick of her lips and another flash of her beautiful teeth sent a new shock wave through my body . . . she longed for me and I longed for her . . . closer . . . closer still she came. I could feel her hot breath on my face and I slowly closed my eyes just as our lips finally met . . . ocean pounding, waves crashing, sun bursting down, white lights and white heat all mashed in my brain and my heart . . . .

Suddenly, it was over . . . I heard a loud, annoying ringing in my ears, drowning out the beach surf, chasing my angel away. The sound cut through my dream-scene and brought me back home. Reality . . . My apartment in downtown Boston. Cold, miserable Boston, in the middle of winter in the middle of another freezing and bitter evening, January 21st. The dead of all seasons . . .

From the darkness of the room, I noted the time on the digital clock. While reaching for the nightlight, I snatched up the notepad I always kept close by. The all-too-alert voice of Captain Tom Blake, Boston Homicide, sounded in my ear as I placed the phone to my head. The room felt icy, dreary, a dull, stark contrast to the beach in my dream.

"Harris? This is Tom down at the station. Sorry to wake you. We have a matter that needs your attention. You need to get down here as soon as possible. There's gonna be a police car outside your place in five minutes."

"What? No hello? No, how ya feeling? Gee Tom, maybe I'm not interested," I stated sharply.

"Oh, sorry Harris. How are you? The car will be there in four minutes. You better get dressed."

"That's better, Tom. But I'm not sure I want in. I just finished the Andrews case and was thinking about taking a little break. You know . . . a vacation. . . . someplace warm and sunny. Away from the killing and the crime and the slush and ice . . . There's this girl I've been thinking about. She's beautiful. Great legs . . . loves the beach, she has this belly ring that . . ."

"You'll want in," Captain Blake said, cutting me off. "Believe me when I tell you. You had better get dressed. You don't want to keep the nice officers waiting outside your place too long. I sent Wallace and Michaels. You know what big fans of yours they are," he said sarcastically.

"Great, Wallace and Michaels." I had been in a few run-ins with the two of them over the years, and was sure that they didn't like me or my unique position on the force. They were strict, old school, play-it-by the numbers cops who wanted no part of my type of police work. It was no accident that Blake was sending the two of them to accompany me to the station.

"Gee Tom, why not just send a South American hit squad to fetch me. I might have a better chance of actually making it to the station alive than with those two."

"South American hit squad. That's kind of funny," Blake said, chuckling. "I'll have to share that with them when they get you here. But you better watch it, I don't think they like you too much. In fact, they were a bit peeved about having to come get you in the first place. They told me to send the drunk tank wagon if I needed you that bad. They said it would make you feel right at home on the way to the station. They also told me that they were too busy to be ferrying around some 'over-priced' eunuch,'" he said, still laughing. "See you in a few minutes, Harris. Don't keep the nice officers waiting." And he hung up.

"Son of a bitch," I said into the empty phone line.

I wrote the time and date in my notepad. I added the names of Wallace and Michaels and Captain Blake. I wondered what had happened this time, knowing that whatever it was wouldn't be pretty. I was only called in on the truly bizarre and dirty jobs, the ones nobody else wanted. It was why the mayor and the police commissioner had created my special position in the first place. I had no permanent position or specific duties. No office I could show up to each and every day. No cute secretary to pour my coffee and ogle while I worked.

Only a direct, exclusive link to Captain Tom Blake.

I received no benefits from the union, and the pay, though excellent, could stop at any time. I was a "non-officer" on special assignment only. My previous cases remained in a well-concealed file.

I finished writing in the notepad and threw on a pair of faded jeans and my Boston Celtics sweatshirt. I splashed water on my face and brushed my teeth. I grabbed my worn, waist-length leather coat from the closet and headed out of my two-room studio. With the notepad tucked in my front pocket, my mind was a thousand miles away. Maybe it was time for a break. The dream embodied such serenity.

Once outside, I reached the bottom of the stairway just as the unmarked police car pulled up. The crisp night air met the slush-covered ground. In winter, Boston was never pretty. Not even at night. A harshness encompassed every nook and cranny of the entire city and wore a person down. No wonder people turned to violence and crime as a way to escape. No wonder there was so much hurt in this big, open wound of a place.

The car skidded to a halt. I stepped over a giant black puddle by the curb and got in. The air inside was hot, stale, and smelled like a fast food restaurant. There were two heads blocking the view up front. The car began to move.

"Boys," I said to officers Wallace and Michaels. Neither turned my way.

"Look," one of them grunted, "it's Magnum P.I." Seemingly inseparable, it was sometimes hard to tell which of them was speaking.

"Very good Michaels," I said, guessing. "Four word sentences. The therapy must be working."

"Screw you, Harris," one of them said.

"Yeah, piss off," the other chimed in.

"Nice of you boys to come out and get me. I would have called a cab but they probably have more important things to do than to ferry guys like me around. It's good to know the department has a couple of top priority men to spare at my beck and call," I said, pushing my luck.

"Oh yeah?" A chorus sounded from the darkness of the front seat.

"Yeah," I answered, just before the car was braked and my face bounced off the headrest in front of me. As we came to a frightening halt, I slammed into the cushion and back into my seat. I felt the hands around my throat before I stopped moving. Officer Michaels had me in the death grip; one in which there was little chance of escaping.

"You wanna be a wise guy? How 'bout I tear that chicken neck in half? Then we'll see who's the funny guy with his head separated from his body," he raged. Leaning back over the seat, his chest was almost on my lap. I could see fire in his eyes and smelled fish cakes on his breath. I felt he was going to break my neck. It was then that I heard the familiar voice from the squawk box, probably saving my life. Captain Tom Blake was calling in, and through my quickly developing haze, I saw the other officer, Wallace, pick up the mic.

"Base to Car 5. Have you picked up our guest?" Blake's voice echoed over the airwaves.

"Car 5 to base. We have him aboard. E.T.A. ten minutes," Wallace answered.

"How's he doing? Is he awake yet?"

"Oh, he's doing fine. He and patrolman Michaels are in the middle of a discussion about department rules on the use of the chokehold as a method of arresting suspects. He's looking forward to working with us on the upcoming case."

"Great, you boys play nice and get your butts in here. I want to see our friend, Harris, as soon as possible. Over."

"Over and out, Captain."

"You better let him go, Bill. The Captain needs him in one piece."

"Sure, sure I will." Michaels grunted before releasing the grip on my throat.

"Thanks a lot. But that'll probably mean a smaller tip for this taxi ride. You boys best learn your manners or you'll be doing this for real someday," I said, rubbing my neck with my right hand. Nobody spoke for the rest of the ride. I knew when I wasn't loved.

After reaching the station, the car stopped. Moving quickly, I jumped from the back, reached into my pocket, and pulled out a dollar bill. Before either officer knew what was happening, I opened the passenger side door and threw the crumpled dollar bill, striking Wallace in the face.

"Here's your tip, cabby. Don't spend it all in one place." I quickly slammed the door and bounded up the front steps of the police station, leaving before the two irate officers had a chance to react. Now it was my turn to laugh.

After a short walk through the quiet, over-lit lobby, I passed the weary looking desk officer on duty. I nodded and he waved me by. I found the fourth door on the right, knocked gently, then entered.

Captain Tom Blake was waiting for me, his back turned, staring out at the bleak, early morning sky.

"Harris, how are you?" he asked, swinging around in his chair. I immediately noticed the anxious look on his face.

"Fine, Tom. What gives?" I didn't like the look.

"Drink? Coffee?" he asked, starting to rise.

"How bad is it? What should I have?"

He paused for a moment. "I'll get the whiskey."

"Great," I moaned softly. I found a seat opposite him and waited while he poured two hefty shots from the Seagram's bottle he kept stashed in his drawer. Leaving the bottle on the cluttered desk, he handed me a glass. I accepted and toasted: "To tanned women in bathing suits. And to the beaches they cavort on."

"To crimeless streets, and the pension I hope to someday collect."

"Skoal." We both drank. After a brief battle, the alcohol settled itself nicely in my empty belly. I poured another for each of us.

"Sorry to rouse you at such an ungodly hour, but we have a problem. What did Wallace and Michaels tell you?"

"Wallace and Michaels? They couldn't tell me where to get a good steak. Those two are useless. I'm surprised they even found their way back to the station without directions."

"Yeah, well . . ."

"Yeah, well nothing, Tom. You should have had them transferred to dog patrol a long time ago."

"Dog officers. Huh, that's another good one. Hell, Harris, you really don't like them, do you?"

"No, I don't. I think they're gung-ho and close-minded and that makes them dangerous. Remember what happened on the Kelso case? I almost got killed because of their lack of judgment. If it wasn't for a lucky bounce, I wouldn't be here drinking all your good whiskey."

"I thought you don't believe in luck," Blake said swirling the whiskey in his glass.

"I don't. There's no room for luck in our business, Tom. We both know that." I drew a slow sip.

"Luck, yeah well, it turned out all right, Harris. You're too good to get caught. I sometimes think you create your own type of luck anyway."

"Whatever, just keep those two away from me. Keep them away from everybody for that matter." With another sip from my glass, I was beginning to feel a little light-headed. "So, what have we got this time?" I asked, unsure if I even wanted to know.

"Murder, Harris."

"I figured that. How many? Where?" I put down my glass.

"Three, across Boston. All women."

"What's the time span?" I asked, pulling out my notepad.

"Meaning?"

"The time span. How many weeks has it been going on? I read the papers. I didn't notice anything unusual."

"Jesus, didn't Wallace and Michaels tell you anything? There is no time span. No 'weeks' at all. They all happened in the last two days," Blake muttered then sighed.

"You're kidding?" I looked directly at him.

"I wish I was."

"Different locations? Same M.O.?"

"You got it. That's why you're here. Strange, huh?"

"I'd say. Can we check the murder sites? Any of them still fresh?" The enticing beach dream poked through my consciousness. Only now, it was dimmer, muted.

"The last one is. The first two victims have already been toe tagged at the morgue. Where do you want to start? I can fill you in on the way . . . " The phone rang at his desk, interrupting him mid-sentence.

"Captain Blake here. You're kidding?" His face took on a pale sheen. "Where? Okay, got it." He hung up the phone and looked at me. "There's been another one, same M.O., near the others."

"Well, I guess that tells us where to begin," I said, rising from my chair. "Sounds like someone's on the rampage," I continued, my dream girl on the beach slipping a million miles away.

The ride to the latest murder scene took exactly eleven minutes. A slight mist fell, making the cold streets slick with ice. While Captain Blake navigated the treacherous streets, he talked. And while he talked, I wrote. He told me all he had learned since the first corpse was found at twenty minutes before midnight, the day before, citing the differences in the victims and the striking similarities linking each of them. It was after the second murder that he began to think of me, he said. It was after the third that the call was made to my apartment.

At 4:37 A.M., the unmarked police car came to a sliding halt outside an uptown hotel called the Provincial. I counted five squad cars already waiting. A yellow DO NOT CROSS-POLICE band had been strung between two iron railings. A lone officer met us at the wind-swept curb and grabbed Blake by the arm. There was a small crowd gathered, perhaps ten or eleven onlookers, but that was it. It was either too early or too late for a big crime scene gathering. We brushed past them and were lead directly to the lobby; a plush, red-carpeted area that reeked of old money and expensive perfume. There were three more police officers stationed in the lobby, all looking somewhat out of place, as their blue uniforms and rain gear clashed with the rich décor of the surroundings. We followed past the lobby to a brass-plated elevator. Another cop held it open. We entered and the door closed behind the four of us. I saw myself in the mirrored back wall, realizing how out of place I suddenly felt. My leather jacket was wet from the mist outside and my hair tussled from the wind. I quickly surmised that, I too, didn't quite fit with the Provincial's plush surroundings.

Well, too damn bad, I sullenly thought to myself. I hadn't asked to be here. I ran my hands through my damp hair and brushed it from my forehead. I felt alert, but slightly out of sync. The time and surroundings, not to mention the two shots of booze at Blake's office, were doing a number on my body clock.

We stopped on the sixth floor. I unzipped my coat as we walked down the corridor, the heavy carpet padding our steps. We came upon room 603. The captain knocked lightly and the door was cautiously opened. Another officer checked us out, then stepped aside. The two officers who had brought us up stayed outside while Blake and I entered the room. I quickly counted five cops including the police photographer, Bob Tolon, inside. Thankfully, Officers Wallace and Michaels were nowhere in sight.

Room 603 was a large, modern suite that must have cost a fortune to occupy. To my left was a huge king-sized bed and two matching night-stands. There was a New Testament Bible on top of one and lamp on the other. The Bible was open. The bed had not been slept in; its spread and blanket were crisp and neat. To my immediate right was a desk and chair set, and beside that, an elegant wet-bar stocked with at least ten different bottles of top-shelf booze. I noticed that the seal to the bottle of gin was broken and about half the liquor was gone. There was an ice bucket on top also. The plastic cover tightly closed, a few cubes left inside. There was a television set on a dark-colored bureau and a large walk-in closet beside that. It was here inside the open closet where I saw the body of victim number four. I had witnessed some weird scenes in my day, but somehow this was the worst.

No wonder I had been called in.

I glanced at Captain Blake and nodded my head. He knew what I wanted and immediately cleared the room. "All right guys, everyone out. Let's get moving. I want ten minutes alone in here. You about through, Bob?" he asked the lab officer taking pictures.

"Yeah, just about," he said, snapping two more shots. "There, that does it."

"Go," he said.

I consulted my notepad and began. "All the women have been found in expensive hotels. All the women have been found with very little indication of a struggle having taken place. Each room is neat in appearance, with no broken lamps, furniture, etc. I am told that no one in adjacent rooms in any of the cases has heard screams or loud noises coming from the murder scenes, so I'm assuming there wasn't a struggle, or if there was, it was minor. Right so far?" I asked, writing frantically.

"Right so far," Blake said.

"The rooms have not been broken into; there has been no sign of forced entry. Neither guests nor hotel employees have seen anyone suspicious hanging around. The only way that anyone even knows about the bodies is that an anonymous call has been made after the murders to the hotel's front desk telling them, and I quote, 'that a sacrifice awaits them,' and then the room number is given. The caller is male, and only stays on the line long enough to use this quote and give the room number. In each case the manager or a hotel employee has gone to the room and found a dead, naked woman hanging upside down. The deaths have all been inside a one mile radius," I said carefully. "All the murders have taken place in the last two days." I finished writing while looking at the corpse again.

"Questions?" Captain Blake asked, coming to my side. I shifted my gaze from the dead woman and looked directly at him.

"Yes. Has there been any sign of rape or sexual assault?"

"The lab won't know for a while, but so far, there doesn't seem to be. I think rape is out."

"Any lifted fingerprints that don't belong?"

"We're checking, but that's going to be nearly

impossible. This is a hotel room and probably hundreds of people have either stayed in it or cleaned it. We've fingerprinted the woman and we're doing the hotel staff now, but it'll be a long shot. No matter how well each room is cleaned daily, there will be latent prints of past guests everywhere, I'm afraid."

"Yeah, you're probably right," I answered. "I'm sure the killer didn't leave much if anything to go on anyway. This was done carefully, skillfully. No noise, no forced entry, and just a brief untraceable phone call describing the whereabouts of the body. This is no dummy we're dealing with," I said somewhat glumly. Something about the body being found upside down continued to tug at my thoughts.

Blake broke in. "Also, in each case, the pocketbooks, jewelry, checkbooks, etc., have been found in the rooms. So robbery is out. Nothing of value has been taken, as far as we can tell."

"The clothes. What about the clothes?" I asked.

"What about them?"

"Where are the victims' clothes? Each has been found naked. The drawers have been found untouched and the personal belongings have been left alone. But what about the clothes each had to have been wearing? Don't tell me that each woman happened to be walking around their hotel rooms stark naked at the very moment that the killer showed up."

"Huh, I never thought of that," Blake said glancing around.

"Yeah, but I did. He took them. That was his souvenir. The money, the wallets, that stuff meant nothing to him. But the clothes somehow did. I have a feeling it has to do with the way each has been found hanging upside down. I want to know what all these women do for a living. I want to know why they're staying in such nice places all by themselves. I see no wedding band on this one but I want to know their marital statuses as well as their ages and where they came from. They're probably out-of-towners if they're staying in hotels," I said looking back at the corpse. "She's a nice looking woman, one who takes care of herself. I'm sure the others are too. You can cut her down now, Tom. I'm all through here. Let's get back to the station, then to a library when it opens. There's one more thing I have to look into," I said before turning away.

"A library? What the hell for?" he asked as we headed towards the door of the suite.

"Not yet. Not here," I said on my way out of the room.

Outside, the night sky was beginning to lighten. The mist was still falling and the clouds looked like gray colored soup. The time was 5:35 in the morning. The longest day of my life was just beginning.

Three hours later, I was sifting through the occult section of the public library. After a brief search, I found what I was looking for. I brought four books over to a large oak table and began to take notes, sometimes lifting whole passages from them. When I was finished, I put the books back on the shelf and took out my phone. I called the station, asked for Captain Tom Blake, and was immediately put through to his office. He answered promptly on the first ring.

"Blake, here. Go."

"Tom, it's Harris. I'm at the library. Any more murders come in?"

"No, none. How'd you do on your end?" he asked.

"Good, I think. You?"

"Pretty good also. You want it over the line?"

"No, better not. I'm coming in," I said. "Before I do though, I want you to check one thing. Do you have the religion of the last woman found?"

"Religion, huh? . . . Wait . . . ah, yeah." I heard papers shuffling. "Her name was Hannah . . . Hannah Ralansky. It says here that she was Jewish. She's a doctor. We found medical papers in a briefcase in the hotel's safe," he read from the report.

"Jewish, huh? What about the others?"

"I have partials on the others. The first woman found was Nancy Chin. No religion if that's what you want, but we're still working on her. The second and third victims are Mary Reilly and Heidi Simpson. Simpson's non-practicing. You know, Agnostic. We just spoke with her father about funeral arrangements. She's going to be cremated. She's a doctor also. We're not sure about the others yet."

"The others are doctors too, I bet. That fits in with what I've been researching."

"Oh yeah? What did you want me to check on?" he asked, his voice perking.

"I noticed that at the last murder scene, the Bible was out on the nightstand. It was open too. This struck me as odd. Most hotels leave them in the drawers. The victim would have had to bring it out to use it. I also noticed that the bottle of gin had been drunk from, and that the ice bucket had been filled. This too struck me as peculiar. You know, a drinker reading the New Testament? Sort of a weird mix."

"Not really," Tom Blake said wearily. It was obvious that he didn't follow my line of reasoning yet.

"Tom, you just said this Hannah Ralansky is Jewish. I really doubt she'd have much interest in a New Testament Bible. I think that the killer took it out. I think there's a reason for it. I want you to re-check the other hotel rooms and see if their Bibles were left out also. Round them up and bring them to the station. Go through each of them page by page. I'm willing to bet it wasn't a coincidence. I'm on my way in. I'm just going to stop at my place for a shower. We have a long day ahead of us. I'll fill you in when I get there," I said before hanging up.

I left the library a little bit wiser than when I went in. I was beginning to gain a handle on the darkness pervading the murders.

At ten-thirty, I was back at the station drinking

black coffee and waiting for Blake, when Officers Wallace and Michaels strolled in and closed the door to the Captain's office. Michaels had a manilla envelope tucked under his huge right arm.

"Hello, Harris," one of them said.

"Good morning, Edwards," the other said cheerily.

I looked up at both of them and smiled. Now, in their civilian clothes, they looked even larger. Both appeared a little tired, yet, seemed glad to see me; an act that was easily detected.

"Hey fellas. What happened? Recess let out early today? I'd offer you something to drink, but I'm afraid that the Captain's all out of hot chocolate and marshmallow." I sipped from my mug and chuckled. For some strange reason, they joined in.

"Funny, Harris."

"Yeah, he's the funny one."

"Thanks, boys. What's up? I mean besides your steroid level." I knew I was pushing my luck again, but didn't really care. Actually, the two of them didn't seem to mind my sarcasm. That made me suspicious. Something was going on. Just then, Captain Blake entered the office.

"Good, you're all here. I'll take that report, Michaels," he said before heading to the coffee maker. He poured himself a cup, then sat behind his desk. "That should be all men," he continued. "Have a nice break."

"Nice break?" I asked. "Don't tell me the gym is closed again."

" 'Nice break' he said," Michaels broke in, laughing.

"Nice break, as in vacation," Wallace said grinning. "We want to thank you, Harris. Because of you we get to take an extra vacation, starting today. It was nice seeing you Harris. Enjoy the slush and snow."

"Yeah, slush and snow. We're off to Cancun. The beach . . . There's women down there who actually go topless. The Captain tells me you like that stuff, although, I find that rather hard to believe."

"The beach? My beach? Oh no you don't. That was my dream. Captain, how could you send these two messenger boys away to my beach?" I asked.

"That will be all, men. Leave the folder. Have a good time," Blake said.

"Bye, Harris."

"Yeah, bye Harris," and they left the office grinning.

"Hell, Tom," I said once they were gone. "I know I said that they're useless, but couldn't you find something they can do? I saw a couple of cars double parked in my neighborhood yesterday. Make them metermaids or something. Just don't send them to my beach."

"Harris, I want them out of your hair. This is the only way. I want your undivided attention on this case. They work here in this division. No matter what, you'd be bumping into them. This way, they're gone," he said picking up the folder left by Michaels. "I have what you want. It's in here. You were right. There was either a New Testament or complete Bible left out in each victim's hotel room, and after going through them, we found that every one had a single passage marked in red pen."

"Really. Now isn't that interesting. I'll bet each victim is a doctor too," I said.

"Yeah, you're right about that also. How'd you know?"

"In a minute. What were the passages? Read me one," I said, reaching for my notepad.

"Okay. This one is from the last victim's room. That would be the Ralansky woman. It's from the New Testament and goes, and I quote, *'In the same way on the outside you appear to people as righteous but on the inside you are full of hypocrisy and wickedness.'* That's from Matthew 23:28," he said looking up. "Want another?"

"The Chin woman. What was circled in her Bible?"

"Let's see, Nancy Chin. Here it is: *'Do not allow a sorceress to live.'* That's from the Old Testament, Exodus 22:18. You want the other two?"

"No, that's enough. I guess that means I'm on the right track," I said. I stopped writing. "I have a few questions, then I'll let you have what I've come up with."

"Shoot."

"Have you found out the cause of death for any of the victims yet?" I held my breath. This was important.

"Well, they're still not sure, but it looks like cardiac arrest brought on my massive heart attacks. Want to know how?" he asked, looking closely at me.

"I know how. By lethal injection. Some sort of toxin was shot into the victims, causing death by embolism. That's why there was no sign of blood in each room. The victims died almost instantly."

"You son of a bitch. Each victim *was* found with a small bruise on the buttocks consistent with a needle entry point," Blake said, shaking his head.

"Next. What was the marital status of the four doctors?" I asked, already knowing the answer to that as well.

"All four were either single or divorced," he read from the folder.

"Right, *handmaidens*," I said under my breath. Things were falling nicely into place.

"What was that you just mumbled?"

"Not yet, Tom. One last question. Doesn't it strike you as funny that all of these women are out of town doctors staying within a one mile radius of each other? Is there some sort of convention around here?"

"Already a step ahead of you on that one, Harris. There is a convention for physicians at The Hilton. Started yesterday. There's over four hundred doctors from all over the country attending."

"Great, plenty of victims to choose from," I muttered. I got out of my chair and poured another cup of coffee.

"All right, Harris, let's have it. It seems you've had a productive morning at the library."

"I have. I guess it all started from the time I saw the victim being hung upside down, the Bible being left out on the table, and the half empty bottle of gin. Something about that struck me as odd. I knew right then that we weren't dealing with some ordinary psycho."

"What do you mean?" he asked.

"I don't know. As I said before, booze and the Bible don't jell. Read it sometime. There's plenty of 'Thou shalt be sent to hell if thou abuses alcohol' stuff in there. It's like oil and water. They don't mix. But it wasn't just that. It was the position of the body. Why hang someone upside down after they are dead?"

"I don't know, but I'm sure you do."

"It's symbolic, that's why. In many beliefs, hanging someone upside down sends that person to eternal damnation. Their head points to Hell so they can never reach salvation. Once I saw that, I knew we were dealing with someone who has some belief in the supernatural. Also, think about this. A·New Testament being read in a Jewish woman's room? Again, not completely logical. I surmised that, given her religion, someone other than the victim had brought that Bible out. I had a feeling there would be some clue contained in it."

"As usual, you've got me riveted. Go on."

"I will. Next, the cause of death also got me thinking. I saw no signs of a physical struggle. No head wounds, no gunshots, no blood. I asked myself how come? Easy. Because death was quick, painless, and very unsuspecting. A real class act."

"Professional?" Blake asked, breaking in.

"Professional, but not like you think. Not committed by a professional killer, but by a professional healer. I think that another doctor did the killing. Someone from that convention is responsible."

"That would explain the needle. Shit, a doctor would have access to needles and drugs and would obviously know which ones to use."

"Right. That would also explain how the killer gained entry into each hotel room. Each victim must have met the killer during the day and had some sort of conversation with him. Or maybe they were old acquaintances. Who knows? I'm sure this isn't the first convention that's ever taken place at The Hilton," I said. "A simple knock on the door would be all that was needed to gain entrance to the rooms. No doctor is going to turn away a familiar face, a colleague, no matter what time it was."

"It all adds up, I guess. By the way, what was that you said earlier? You mumbled 'handmaidens' when I told you each woman's marital status?"

"Oh, that? The term 'handmaidens' goes back to the Salem Witch Trials in the sixteen hundreds. Handmaidens or single women who were financially independent were usually the first ones suspected of being in league with the devil. In fact, handmaidens and midwives made up the majority of women hung in the gallows. I'm assuming the killer, in his distorted mind, equated midwifery to modern medicine or a female doctor. Again, the only reason I even got on that particular track was the position of the body, with her head hanging upside down. If she had been found right side up or laying on the floor I wouldn't have gotten this feeling. It was a hunch and I went with it."

"What about the missing clothes?"

"That, I'm not sure about yet. I still have some holes in the story to sort out. But I'm close."

"So what we have, you're saying, is some thought-disordered doctor who thinks he's a Puritan, acting on behalf of God?"

"Yeah, something like that. For some reason he's singling out unmarried, female doctors. He believes they're evil. That's why he's circling certain passages of the Bible. He's telling us what he's doing and why he's doing it. He's sending a message, thus rationalizing the killings. He thinks God is on his side and what he's doing is right."

"What a sickening way to think. He's obviously a very unstable person."

"Highly. He has distorted reality badly enough to believe he's doing something good. He won't stop either. He feels he is doing humanity a favor," I stated, putting away the notepad.

"What are we going to do about it? I can't storm the convention center. That would rouse the killer's suspicion, probably sending him undergound," Blake said.

"Yeah, you're right, you can't. The killer would see a lot of cops around and take his business elsewhere. Remember, this man is probably a doctor and this makes him smart. We have to be very careful. Very low key," I said, thinking aloud.

"So?" Blake asked, rising from his chair.

"So, I guess I'm going to a convention. My mother always wanted me to be a doctor," I quipped. "She'll be happy to learn that I joined the profession." The time was 11:36 A.M.

A tall, well-dressed man casually strolls down the hallway of an upscale hotel. In his right hand he carries a small black medical bag. He passes many rooms, glancing at the numbers on each door, and stops when he reaches room 603. He pauses a moment and looks around, checking to see whether anyone else is in the hallway. Satisfied that the area is deserted, he knocks gently on the door. After a brief moment or two, the muffled sound of a woman calls out from inside the room. He answers her, and the door opens just enough for her to peek outside and view her visitor. She opens the door, inviting the tall man inside.

Dressed in designer jeans and a black top, she is an attractive woman with shoulder-length blonde hair and a shapely figure. Although she looks surprised— even puzzled — to see him, she smiles and shakes his hand. Clearly, she is at ease with him.

The pair engage in polite small talk, like two acquaintances who haven't seen each other in months, maybe years. She offers him a drink, which he declines. As he places the medical bag on a chair by the door, she walks over to the wet-bar in the room, puts ice in a glass, and pours herself a drink. She smiles and raises her glass to him before taking a sip. She puts the glass back down, comes out from behind the bar and sits on the barstool set up in front of it. She is smiling and seems happy to catch up on old times.

The talking continues for a short while, but the woman's expression gradually changes. Her visitor's words seem to unsettle her. She isn't smiling anymore and seems unsure where to place her hands. She stammers for words.

The man steps closer to the bar where the woman is sitting. She takes another sip from her drink and then tries to get up from the barstool, as if to get something left in another part of the room. She turns her head for a brief moment and scans the room. The man quietly and expertly slips on a pair of black leather gloves. He reaches out his left hand and firmly pushes her back down.

Her eyes widen as she reaches up to push him away. He is too strong. As she opens her mouth to scream, his gloved hand covers her lips, and she is unable to utter any sound except a muffled cry. Her eyes flash wider as panic rises like a wave inside her.

The man's right hand emerges from inside his jacket pocket. He clutches a shiny hypodermic needle, its point dripping with a clear fluid. The woman reaches out her left arm to push him away, but he thrusts the needle under her arm, penetrating the pliable flesh of her armpit. He depresses the syringe, sending poison into her body. Immediately, the woman's expression glazes over with horror. Her arm falls limp and her eyes begin to roll up into her head. She slumps, drugged and motionless, on the shoulder of the man.

He gently puts her down on the carpet, leaving her there for a moment. He walks over to the nightstand beside the bed and pulls out a Bible. He flips through the pages, seeming to know where to stop. He walks back to the dying woman and stands over her with the Bible in his hands. Her head is slowly rolling from side to side. She seems to be gasping for air. He gets to a certain page, picks out a passage and reads it aloud: "In the same way on the outside you appear to people as righteous but on the inside you are full of hypocrisy and wickedness."

He then reaches into his coat pocket, pulls out a pen and underlines the passage. He walks the Bible back over to the nightstand, turns the pages and places it back on top of it.

After that, he returns to the woman and removes her clothes, placing the garments in a neat pile on the floor. He drags the body over to the large walk-in closet opposite the bed. From his medical bag, he pulls out some rope. He binds her hands and her feet. He takes another piece of longer rope and throws it over the pole in the closet. He takes this rope and ties it to the noose at her feet. He begins to pull until her entire body is hanging upside down inside the closet. He ties off the rope to secure her, retrieves the clothes he has taken from her and stuffs them into his medical bag. The man glances around the room again. Ignoring the dead woman hanging in the closet, he exits the room. When he reaches the end of the long hallway, he disappears through a doorway.

The woman continues swinging slightly from her cradle of death, her body gently rocking, her stare glazed and lifeless.

Two hours after leaving Captain Blake's office, I entered The Hilton Convention Center in downtown Boston. Compliments of the Boston Police Department, my name had made it on the guest list. Seems going to med school was overrated as I went from undercover policeman to Dr. Harris Edwards in two short hours. At the check-in table I was given a guest pass and a name tag. The lobby was already filled with men wearing expensive suits and women in expensive dresses. I was glad that I had been able to rescue my one and only sports jacket and dress slacks from the back of my bedroom closet. However, I did have to stop and buy a pair of shoes to compliment the outfit. I had to admit that my look did fit in. Still, 'disguise' and all, I was feeling a bit self-conscious.

On another table, I picked up a daily itinerary. There were lectures and guest speakers listed throughout the day. I also noticed that there was a cocktail hour starting at two o'clock and I quickly surmised that this was something more my speed, so I ambled over to the entrance of the lounge. Once inside, I noticed that other doctors were thinking along the same lines. The place was nearly filled, despite the early afternoon hour.

It was a typical hotel bar. Dim lights, rich décor, and brass everything. I slid past a couple of "colleagues" and asked one of the busy bartenders if he had been on duty the day before. He shook his head, then pointed to a co-worker at the other end of the bar.

"Nope, but she was," he said before taking another order.

"Thanks." I pushed my way towards her and ordered a drink. A moment later she was back.

"Here you go," the bartender said to me. She was a tall, wholesome looking redhead, about thirty years of age.

"Thanks, how much?" I asked, pushing a twenty dollar bill her way.

"Open bar 'til four, doctor," she said, smiling.

"Doctor, huh? Oh, yeah. Here, keep it anyway. Remember my face when the rush is on."

"I'll remember your face in my dreams tonight," she said, first looking at the money then me. "I'm Kim. Holler if you need anything," she said sweetly.

"I'm Harris. . . . I mean Doctor Harris Edwards." I extended my hand over the bar.

"Nice to meet you, Dr. Harris."

"Same here."

"Funny. You don't look like a doctor."

"Really?" I asked, cautiously. The self-conscious feeling was growing.

"Yeah, you're too cute," she said, lowering her voice. "The rest of these people . . . They're doctors. Something is different about you."

"Is that so?"

"Yeah, you know they look stuffy, made up, I don't know . . . Stiff somehow. You have a relaxed look about you."

"Relaxed, huh?" I asked, sipping my drink. I felt anything but.

"Yeah, casual-like. Nice."

"I still don't get you."

"Not uptight." The smile remained on her pretty face. I realized that I liked it there and I also realized that I liked looking at it. A lot.

"Hmmm."

"You look a bit out of place. Hold on. I'll be right back. Duty calls," and with that she was gone. I watched her efficiently move around the bar, filling drink glasses and taking more orders. She was back in a minute. The smile never left her face.

"So, what were we talking about?"

"You said I looked a bit out of place. But that I wasn't uptight. What do you mean by uptight?"

"Uptight . . . stiff. . . . I don't know how to explain it. Now take yesterday for example. There was this guy. Wow . . . What a character," Kim said shaking her head. "A real piece of work. One uptight individual."

"Oh yeah? How so?" I asked.

"Oh, I probably shouldn't say," she said lowering her voice.

I wondered how many bartenders I had interviewed over the years. I wondered how small the number of leads was that I actually had gotten from these hearty souls who saw everything but kept their mouths shut, like they had taken some sacred oath to never snitch on their fellow man and to take no sides in a disagreement.

"Tell me," I gently prodded.

"Why should I?" she teased and glanced around.

"So I won't act like him. So you don't think I'm some uptight individual and scare you away."

"You're funny. I like you." Suddenly, she walked to the waitress station at the far end of the bar. She signaled for me to join her. I took my drink and followed.

"Go ahead."

"Well, there was this one guy, this doctor in here yesterday. He was weird, strange-like."

"Really? Why do you say that?"

"I don't know. He looked okay, but he talked kind of funny," she said softly. "He gave me the creeps after a while." Kim seemed to shudder at the thought of him.

"How? What do you mean by, 'he talked funny'?"

"You know, weird. It wasn't actually the talking, but the way he talked. His . . . how do you say it? His diction was different. He didn't drink either. He just sat here all afternoon drinking ginger ale. The place was dead. Lots of lectures going on, I guess. He had to have been here for two hours. It seemed more like ten, if you want the truth."

"Interesting," I said. I wondered if this could be my man. "Tell me, Kim, what do you mean 'his diction was weird'?"

"I don't know . . . his words . . . his tone of voice. Ah, he said things like *tavern*. What was the other thing? Ummm, . . . *libation*. He called this place a tavern and he asked for a non-alcoholic libation. He also asked me if I was *spoken for*. Spoken for? What the hell is that? Who says stuff like that in this day and age?"

I may have him, I suddenly thought to myself. It may be him. It had to be. It was all connected. The handmaidens, the midwifery business in the Bible passages found in the dead woman's rooms. He's a crusader. Some type of Middle Ages warrior, right down to the fancy Old World language he was using. "That does sound weird. Was he a doctor?" I asked, putting down my drink.

"I think he was . . . yeah sure. . . . A couple of other doctors were in and out while he was here. One woman, a pretty oriental woman said hello and stopped to speak with him for a few. She seemed to know him. She came through to use the restroom."

An oriental woman. That might be Nancy Chin. Victim number one.

"Can you describe him?" I asked. I might be getting close.

"No!" Kim suddenly said, her eyes widening.

"What?" I asked, taken aback.

"No, I can't," she said, her gaze looking past my right shoulder.

"He's here, isn't he?" I said, sensing the root of her sudden change of demeanor.

"Just walked in . . . The tall thin man with the grey beard . . . Look, I gotta get back to work." Gone was the smile from before.

"Me too," I muttered under my breath. "How about dinner sometime?"

"You know where to find me, Dr. Harris who ain't no doctor."

"Thanks Kim."

"Ah huh." And with that she was gone.

I spun in the direction of the entrance, just as the tall man with the grey beard sat down at one of the small tables lining the back wall of the lounge. An older waitress scurried over and took his order. She came my way and squeezed past me, obviously not happy at where I was standing. Seems I was in her way.

"Excuse me," she said in a grumpy voice.

"Let me guess. A ginger ale," I said, excusing myself.

"You get the door prize." She called out the order. It was delivered quickly by my new friend Kim.

"Now, why would anyone hang around a bar and sip soft-drinks?" I asked.

"Why does anyone do anything?" she said before leaving with the drink on her tray.

"Good point," I said to her fleeting backside.

I continued to watch him for a few moments, trying to formulate my plan of attack. Information ran through my head. The cause of death, the victims, the upside down hanging in the closet, the Bible passages, the clothes taken for souvenirs. I stood for another few seconds trying to get a feel for my instincts. I suddenly noticed that he was not wearing a name-tag like the rest of us in the lounge. I decided the direct approach was as good as any. I sauntered over to his table, drink still in hand.

"Excuse me. Dr. Waters, is it?" I said, feigning recognition. "Remember me? . . . Edwards. . . . Harris Edwards from New York."

"Sorry . . . Wrong person," he said glancing up to me. He looked tired. His eyes were like black holes.

"Are you sure?"

"Young man . . . Dr. Edwards," he said reading my name-tag. "I don't know all that the world has to offer, but I do know my own name."

"Hmm. . . . Sorry. May I sit anyway?" I nodded to the chair opposite him.

"Yes. Someplace else."

"It's just that I don't know anyone else here today. It's my first time in Boston." I pressed on.

"You're lucky. I live here . . . Now go away."

"It's just that I feel a little funny . . . you know . . . a little bit out of place."

"You look out of place."

"Really? You're the second person to tell me that in the past few minutes."

"Who was the first?"

I paused for a moment. I decided to try something. "The *innkeeper* behind the bar," I said, stressing the word innkeeper. His eyes widened momentarily, then narrowed. He peered towards the front of the lounge, saw Kim the bartender, and shook his head. "The *wench*," he said, almost spitting out the words.

"Yeah, her," I agreed.

"Sit."

"Thank you." I placed my drink on the table

and sat down. I reached across and extended my right hand. "Dr. Harris Edwards. New York."

"Dr. Fletcher James. Charmed." He briefly shook my hand.

"Can I buy you a drink, Dr. James?"

"A drink? I haven't had a drink in two years. Poison it is. Slow death to no place."

"Can I buy you one anyway? There are worse ways to go."

"Are there? Name one."

"One could die of boredom . . . Or how about loneliness? That to me is worse than poison."

"Hmm. Perhaps you're right." He closed his eyes, deep in thought. A strange look struck his face. He seemed to be revisiting some distant memory. It was an eerie look. A few moments later he was back. "Sure, a drink would be fine. I'll have whatever you're having."

"Excellent." I signaled to the waitress. She quickly came to the table. "Excuse me, *barmaid*. I would like two Crown Royals. Straight up."

"Yes, *squire*," she said, rolling her eyes. I watched her walk away, hoping my choice of words was not lost on my companion.

"Barmaid? Innkeeper? You have an interesting

vocabulary," James said, pushing away his glass of ginger ale.

"Do I? I never noticed."

"Sure you do. Tell me. Why do you speak like that?"

"Like what?"

"Like that. You use old phrases. Words that have been out of use for a long time."

"Oh . . . I don't know. It's just that I have always liked old things. Different times perhaps . . . The old ways . . . Maybe I'm a reincarnated blacksmith or something."

"Or a doctor perhaps."

"Yes . . . maybe I was a doctor in some past life. . . . I often have this dream about a beach. . . . maybe I was a doctor on a pirate ship." I smiled.

James joined me with a grin of his own. "Hmm. Now wouldn't that be rewarding." The smile was almost gruesome.

"How so?"

"Well, back then, there was little of today's so-called modern medicine techniques. Back then, it was more a slice and dice routine. If you had an infection, they burned it out of you. Or put maggots in your wound to eat the infection. If you had a bullet wound, they cut off your arm.

Doctors back then, were nothing more than skilled carpenters. Taking the Hippocratic Oath meant that you owned your own handsaw."

Our drinks arrived. They were ignored. The lounge was filling up at a rapid pace.

"That does not sound like the good 'ole days," I said, watching Dr. James. He had a strange, hypnotic way of speaking. Kim was right. He was capable of giving a person the creeps.

"Oh, but it was. Things were simple then. Black and white with no in between. Healers were healers and killers were killers . . . healers went on to become doctors. Killers went to the gallows. Now times have changed."

"Healers? . . . Killers? I don't understand."

"You wouldn't. You're too young." He picked up his drink and sipped from the heavy glass. He closed his eyes again and savored the whiskey's taste. "Now, I remember why I stopped drinking. Anything this good must be bad for you."

Nervously, I joined him. "What's wrong with being bad?"

"Nothing . . . Nothing at all. It's just easier than being good . . . I detest anything easy." He drained his glass and set it down between us. He paused for a moment. A new idea seemed to come to him. "I like you, Dr. Edwards. I actually think I like you. Would you like to hear a story?"

"A story? Sure. You have me intrigued."

"It's a rather sad tale, I'm afraid. Not too long a tale . . . but sad just the same."

"Well, if you would rather not . . . I understand." I too drained my glass. I signaled to the waitress to order us another round. She nodded when she saw me.

"No. . . . No it's okay. It might feel good to let it out for a change."

"Go ahead, Dr. James."

"Once upon a time a very happy man met a very beautiful . . . very special girl. And that girl was taken away from that man in a way that is — even in this cruel world — unfair." He stopped for a moment, seeming to compose himself. I didn't say a word. I felt like I needed for him to tell me what was on his mind. It was a strange situation I found myself in, sitting with a possible serial killer — who was about to tell me some sob story about an old girlfriend breaking up with him. How quaint. But for once, I kept my smart mouth shut and listened.

"So this happy, successful man met the love of his life, married her and lived a storybook existence until one day-something happened and it came to a smashing halt."

"Go on." The drinks came. Again they were ignored.

"Thank you. One day the girl got sick and needed to go to the doctor's office. Woman stuff . . . some pain, some bleeding . . . nothing major. Or so she thought. But when this young girl got there, the doctor was very busy with her other patients and didn't spend the proper amount of time with the girl. So the girl was seen briefly and told to relax in the waiting room. And there the pain got worse and worse. But being a brave and patient girl, she did not complain or make a stink, figuring there were others ahead of her who were having just as much pain as she was. So she waited. And she waited some more. Until finally her belly felt like it was going to burst . . . and burst it did. She started to bleed profusely . . . started bleeding . . . right there in that crowded waiting room. And before anything could be done, she died. She died on the same chair she was told to wait in. She died and lost the baby inside of her, the one she didn't even know she was carrying. And a man, a decent, successful, happy man became a widower and an 'almost father' in the span of about 45 minutes." Dr. James stopped. He took a deep breath and closed his eyes again. When he opened them, he looked directly into mine. There was a look in them that sent my bowels twisting in my belly.

"Some story, huh?" He almost smiled again.

"Unreal. Sorry. I take it that was your wife and your unborn baby in that story."

"Uh huh. My wife . . . my beautiful wife who never hurt a soul in her life. Died because some fucking witch doctor was too busy to take the time to check her out in the proper fashion . . . Disgraceful . . . Disgraceful . . . and totally avoidable. A fucking waste . . . An avoidable waste of human life."

I sipped my fresh drink and stared back at him. "I don't know what to say."

"Say nothing. There is no need. Your eyes show the compassion in your soul. It's enough you listened. It's enough you took a moment out of your busy life and listened. Sometimes that's enough."

"Jesus. Then what happened?"

"What happened? I buried her . . . I buried both of them and I went on living in a world that had suddenly turned from beauty into eternal hell. Eternal hell because one God-forsaken bitch-doctor didn't take the time . . . didn't take the time to look past her own stupidity and incompetent ways. That fucking creature . . . If I had been in that office that day, I swear I would have . . ." His words fell off before finishing.

"Would have what?" I pressed. I needed him to say it.

"I would have . . . ahhhh . . . nothing . . . I would have been too overcome with grief to even yell at her and her staff . . . It was a mistake . . . an awful mistake, but a mistake is a mistake. We all make them from time to time." His voice trailed off. He seemed able to compose himself. He looked around the room. I had forgotten where we even were.

"You know. It's getting too packed in here. What do you say we take this discussion someplace else? It's too crowded for my taste. There's something I would like to show you." he said.

"Sure. Where?"

"My room. I'm staying here at the hotel. I believe there is some more of this evil stuff upstairs," he said pointing to his whiskey glass. "Maybe we could have another drink and talk some more of the old ways?"

"All right. What room is it? I have a couple of phone calls to make. I can be there in, say, fifteen to twenty minutes, tops."

"1023. Don't be long. What I have to show you is very special."

"I won't be. Room 1023, right? See you in a few." I watched him get up from the table and leave the lounge. I sat for another few minutes and drained the rest of my drink, before heading back to the bar. Through the assembled crowd, I signaled for Kim, the bartender. She immediately headed back down to the waitress station. I followed. I pulled a pen from my pocket and grabbed a cocktail napkin off the bar. I wrote down Captain Tom Blake's number at the station. I added room 1023. I handed it to her.

"What time do you get off?"

"Not until six."

"This is the number of a very important person. If I'm not back in here by five o'clock, I want you to call him and tell him I'm in this room at this hotel."

"You're a cop. I knew it. I knew you were no doctor."

"You were right. Remember. Five o'clock. Call

him and tell him who you are and where I am. He'll know what to do."

"Okay, handsome."

"Thanks, Kim. I owe you one."

"I'm going to hold you to that," she said smiling. I watched her stuff the note into her front pocket, wondering how she would look on a beach, realizing, probably pretty great. I turned and waited ten minutes before heading up to room 1023. Not knowing what awaited me there. Not realizing that I might have seen my last beach, in this life anyway.

After a short elevator ride, I arrived on the tenth floor. I walked down a long corridor and found James' room. I put my ear to the door, but heard nothing unusual. I knocked and a moment later, the door opened. However, it wasn't Dr. James who answered but instead a very beautiful Asian woman. Flabbergasted, I started to walk away.

"Sorry, wrong room," I mumbled and turned.

"Hold it. Dr. Harris Edwards, correct?"

"Ah, yes." I stopped.

"We've been expecting you. Come on in."

"Oh, I'm sorry. I didn't know that Dr. James was having guests."

"Oh, he's not. It's just the three of us. He called me on the phone and asked me to come up. I'm staying on the third floor. We used to work together. He said he had someone I needed to meet. He stepped out for a minute. I'm Ivy. Dr. Ivy Ling."

"Harris, Dr. Harris Edwards from New York." We shook hands. Dr. Ling stepped aside and I entered.

"Drink?"

"Please. Whiskey, rocks if you have it."

"I have it," she said walking towards the bar. She made mine and freshened hers, which was already poured. I watched her, admiring the view. She was wearing tight black slacks and a beige, knit sweater. Her figure was perfect. In fact, she was one of the most beautiful woman I had ever seen.

"Here you go."

"Thanks." I accepted and drank. I couldn't keep my eyes off of her.

"So, what brings you to Boston?"

"The convention. I've never been to one. I've only been practicing medicine for two years. This is my first real vacation," I lied.

"Yes, it is exciting isn't it? This is my third year coming. There's so many interesting people."

"Where do you practice?"

"Here in the city. I run a women's clinic on Boylston Street."

"It must be very rewarding."

"Yes, it is. I love working with people. Most women come to me under dire circumstances. I feel like I am helping them in difficult times."

"How do you know Dr. James?" I asked, sipping my drink.

"Oh, I interned under him at the university. I was lucky. It was his last year in medicine."

"Really? So he's retired?"

"Yes, he is. It's too bad. He was a great doctor."

"I didn't know he was through practicing medicine. What would he be doing here at the convention, I wonder?"

"I don't know. It's funny. I didn't even know he was here until he called me. I was surprised. We haven't spoken in two or three years. I was happy to hear his voice on the phone."

"I'll bet. How did he know where you were staying?"

"Oh, I stay here every year. I also leave my name at the front desk in case someone needs to reach me," she said.

"What did he say about me?"

"He called and said to come up for a drink. He said that he had bumped into a younger version of himself and that I just had to meet you." She smiled. "How could I resist such an invitation?" Her eyes held a powerful, magnetic stare. I could feel them pulling me towards her. We stood looking at each other for a long moment. I cleared my throat and sipped from my drink. I heard a key in the door behind me, and a moment later Dr. Fletcher James entered the room, carrying a brown shopping bag.

"Ah, good. Everyone's here. I think it's time for a little party." He looked frazzled. Gone was the brash demeanor present in the hotel lounge. There was an edge in his voice that I didn't like. I suddenly wished that I had brought my gun. I glanced at my watch. It was only 3:58.

"A party? Gee, there's only three of us," Dr. Ling answered lightly. I detected no nervousness in her voice. It was obvious that she trusted James. If only she knew what I suspected.

"Yes, a party. And guess what, Ivy? You are the guest of honor," he said glancing her way.

"I am? What for?"

"Oh, that's easy. We are going to celebrate all the good work you've done in the past. Isn't she lovely, Dr. Edwards? Can you imagine a woman so beautiful and not spoken for? It's a sin really." He was still looking at Ling. He casually placed the chain on the door and set down the bag.

"Yes, she is lovely," I agreed, scanning the room. From here, I was unable to see the rest of the suite. "In fact, I was just about to ask Dr. Ling if she would like to grab an early dinner with me. Perhaps we could come back later." I suddenly felt like a caged animal. I didn't like being here without my gun.

"You were?" Ling questioned. The smile on her face grew.

"Nonsense," James broke in tersely. "You can have dinner later. I insist."

"I'm not hungry. Not yet anyway. But I may take you up on your offer later, Dr. Edwards."

"Fine."

"Now, Harris, would you make me one of those wonderful drinks you have there? Dr. Ling and I are going into the other room for just a minute. Wait here and when I call, you can bring it in," James said forcing a smile. "Come, Ivy. I want to show you something." He left the room carrying the bag and she followed.

"Sure. Sure thing," I said, trying to sound relaxed. I didn't like what was happening, but had little choice except to stay. I could not leave her with him. I searched the room but found no phone. The bastard had probably ripped it out of the wall. I heard the TV in the other room switch on, a little too loudly. I walked to the bar and made another drink.

A minute passed, then another. The only sounds coming from the bedroom emanated from the television; a diet soft drink commercial, then someone who sounded like Dr. Phil. I looked at my watch; they had been in there almost five minutes. One more and I was going in. I had no plan, but knew I could probably take James one on one. He was bigger, but older by twenty years. I slipped off my sport coat and slung it across the bar. Just as I was about to rush the room, I heard the voice of Ivy Ling call me into the bedroom. Her voice held an edge of fear. I downed my drink, snatched up the doctor's and walked towards the room. If needed, the heavy rock glass would serve as a weapon.

Upon reaching the closed door, I knocked. The TV was turned down. After a moment James instructed me to enter. I took a deep breath, reminding myself that the doctor thought of me as a friend. I stepped inside the room into a scene straight out of some Gothic horror novel. I nearly dropped the glass.

The first thing I saw was Dr. James sitting on the bed, his hair in disarray, a constricted look on his face. He suddenly appeared older, much older, than when we first met less than an hour ago. His eyes were wide, frozen into some perverted stare. His mouth was tightly closed; his lips clamped like a vice. His nostrils were flared, etching lines around the bridge of his nose. He looked like he was in a trance, a dark, evil trance. There was a gun in his right hand, pointed in the direction of the closet. There was an open Bible on his lap. I nearly gasped at the sight of him. He was staring straight ahead. It took all I had to peel my eyes from him, toward the object of his attention. I saw Dr. Ivy Ling. I squeezed the rock glass in my hand. It was the only thing that kept me from prematurely going after James.

Naked, Ling was hung upside down; her feet latched to the pole in the closet. Her hands were tied at her waist, just like the other victims. Her eyes blinked slow and deliberate. Her black hair fell, forming an elaborate fan on the thick, white carpet. I saw no blood, no signs of a struggle. Two complete woman's outfits were slung from hangers on both sides of her. Four in all, each representing a dead or soon to be dead woman. The slacks and sweater Ling had been wearing were closest to her. They too were upside down, resembling lifeless scarecrows. In front of each garment was a burning candle. So this is what he did with the victims' clothes; the bastard took them to build an altar out of his conquests.

The entire scene resembled some bizarre pagan celebration. A mixture of anger and revulsion rose up inside of me. I wanted to kill him. I wanted to throttle his face with my bare fists. Yet, James held the gun and there was little I could do. I slowed my breathing to remain calm. A quick assessment of the situation produced my next plan of action.

He said that he had bumped into a younger version of himself, Dr. Ling had recounted earlier. Recovering quickly, I turned and forced a sinister smile.

"What do you think of my handy work, Dr. Edwards?" James said coolly.

"Nice. An improvement actually." I walked over to the closet and knelt down. There was terror in Ling's glazed eyes. I realized she had been drugged. *"Wench,"* I said disgustedly. Knowing he was watching my every move, I aimed carefully and spat on her chest. *"Sorceress.* You evil bitch. You're all the same." Behind me, James cackled. I stood and turned towards him.

"Is she drugged?"

"Yes."

"Lethally?"

"No."

"Let's kill her now," I said. "Slowly."

"In due time, Dr. Edwards . . . In due time." The gun was resting in his hand. His eyes were like poison darts. I heard Ling moan.

"How are we going to do it?" I asked.

"The bag. Get it." He motioned to the brown shopping bag sitting on a nightstand beside the bed. I cautiously walked over to it. James' glare never left Ling. I reached inside and brought out a capped hypodermic needle.

"What is it?" I asked.

"Death. That's what it is." James chuckled. "Jab a human and death occurs in less than three minutes."

"Is it traceable?"

"Hardly. It makes the victim look like she has

suffered a major heart attack. However, this bitch has no heart. So I rather doubt that it would even harm her."

"Really? Why is that?"

"She's nothing but a butcher."

"What do you mean?"

"A butcher. She runs a women's clinic. You don't have to be a genius to know what goes on inside one of those places."

"Ah, I see." Now it all made sense. Ling performed abortions. In his stilted state of mind, he saw her as evil.

"Witch," he said angrily.

"Let's do it." I needed to get close to James. It was the only way that I could subdue him. I started to walk towards Ling again. Shaking the Bible from his lap, James got off the bed and followed. I could feel the gun pointed at my back.

A moment later we were standing in front of Dr. Ling. Her face was flushed from being hung upside down. She appeared too drugged to realize what was happening. I still had the needle, but no real plan. James remained behind me. He seemed to sense my hesitance.

"What are you waiting for? Jab her."

"I don't know if I can do it."

"Do it. She's nothing but an evil sorceress. You'll be doing the world a favor . . . her a favor. You'll be sending her to Hell. It's where she wants to go. It's where she belongs." I heard the hammer of the gun click. "Do it, or join her in eternal damnation." I could feel the cold steel of the gun at my scalp. "You have five seconds to make up your mind. God is waiting."

My mind raced. The needle was my only chance, but I knew I'd never get the chance to spin and use it on James. Slowly, I uncapped the needle and dropped the covering to the floor. I realized I was probably going to die. A vision of the girl on the beach floated through my thoughts. Although never sure about living in Boston, I was certain that I didn't want to die here.

"Where should I stick her?" I asked, motioning to Ling.

"Under the arm. It's harder to trace there."

"All right," I said. I crouched down to the naked doctor. The gun at the back of my head followed with steady pressure. Seeing no way out, however suicidal it was, I was going to have to reach back and hit James with the deadly needle. I took a deep breath, poising myself for the attack. What I needed was a diversion.

What I got was a miracle. For just then, help arrived from an unlikely source.

Suddenly, from outside the room, I heard the door to the suite burst open and the chain snap in its saddle. A loud, familiar voice called out: "Room Service!" The muffled sound of heavy footsteps followed. The gun momentarily left my head and I heard James cry out, "What the hell?"

Dr. Ling moaned and the door to the bedroom was thrown open. I quickly sprang from the crouch I was in. I thrust my head up and into James' chin, just as the gun went off. I felt my head smash into his jaw and heard a dull thud along with the reverberating gunshot. I was nearly knocked unconscious from the shattering blow to my head, wondering all the while if I had been shot. I reached back and rammed the needle into James' soft thigh and twisted it hard just as we were both falling. I landed on top of him, my back on his chest, my eyes staring straight up at the ceiling. Beneath me, his body went limp. The room started spinning. In a fuzzy blur, I saw two large objects hovering over me, both dressed in funny looking uniforms. Through my swimming vision, Officers Wallace and Michaels were holding guns and grinning broadly. I tried to raise a smile, but even that hurt.

I heard one say to the other: "See, he's always laying down on the job." Then I passed out.

Twenty minutes later, I was sitting on the hotel bed with an ice pack on my throbbing head. To my left was the still shape of Dr. James. To my right, in a wooden chair, a very shaken Dr. Ling sat sipping something from a glass. A hotel bathrobe had been draped over her shoulders. I heard Captain Tom Blake from the outer room as he was speaking to Wallace and Michaels in an excited voice. After the brief conversation was over, he strolled into the bedroom with a drink in his hand.

"Tough day at the office, Doctor?"

I accepted the drink and smiled slowly. "Kind of."

"You're lucky. If you weren't such a charming, impressionable young man, you might not be drinking that free whiskey."

"What do you mean?"

"It seems that you made quite an impression on that gorgeous bartender downstairs. I just talked to her. She was worried about you. She said that you wanted her to wait until five o'clock to call us. However, she got concerned and called us earlier."

"Why?" I asked.

"Well, after you left her downstairs, she saw the good doctor over there come back through the lounge. She knew you were going up to his room. She saw him carrying a bag and got nervous. In fact, when she saw him come back, she thought you might be already dead. She was smart though. She called us right away. It just so happens that I had two officers stationed at the hotel already. Both dressed as bellhops." Blake was smiling now. It was obvious that he was enjoying this on some level.

"Wallace and Michaels," I said. That explained the peculiar dress.

"Yup, Wallace and Michaels. The world's largest set of bellboys."

"I thought you sent them on vacation," I said, sipping my whiskey.

"Oh that. That was just a front. I needed them to stay close to you, but I couldn't let you know they were around. I know they get on your nerves. I didn't want you distracted. So, I made up all that beach stuff and vacation talk. You gave me the idea actually. You kept talking about some girl . . . some beach. They probably saved your life. Them and that beautiful creature working the downstairs bar."

"Unreal . . . What about him?" I motioned to a limp Dr. James.

"Oh, he's dead. Died when you hit him with that needle. Sick bastard."

"Her?" I turned my attention to Dr. Ling.

"She's okay. She's still a little bit out of it. She's gonna be fine in a couple of hours."

"Great. Am I finished here or what?" I drained the rest of my drink.

"For now. Sure."

"I guess I gotta go in and thank Wallace and Michaels. That won't be easy." I rubbed a large knot on my head. "Maybe I should have let Dr. James shoot me." Blake smiled. I painfully got up from the bed and began walking unsteadily from the room. I noticed the Bible on the floor. I picked it up and saw that a page had been folded over and a passage had been circled in red pen. It was from Chronicles 16:22 and read: *"Do not touch my anointed ones; do my prophets no harm."* Shaking my head, I flung it on the bed and quietly left the room.

In the living room, looking quite ridiculous in their bellhop uniforms, the two officers were waiting for me. Both were grinning.

"Wallace and Michaels, I just want to thank you guys for coming when you did. You really saved my ass."

"No problem, Edwards," one of them said.

"Yeah, we figured you'd need help ... per usual," the other chimed in. Both chuckled.

"Right. Oh, and one more thing."

"Yes?" Wallace asked.

"What is it?" Michaels responded.

"Since you're still dressed like that, don't forget my bags, Wallace. Oh, and Michaels, could you run down and hail me a cab? I want to get to the airport. Hurry along. There'll be a good tip in it for both of you."

Two days later, on a beach far away from the cold streets of Boston, a vision appeared. A woman was walking towards me, a beautiful woman, wearing a very revealing bathing suit. She was already tanned, her reddish-brown hair reflecting the bright sunshine. Her breasts were full, her body lean. There was a smile on her face, a smile of hunger and passion. In her hands were two drinks. She handed me one and when she kissed me lightly on the lips, this time, the phone didn't ring, waking me in the dead of night. This time there really was no booking rooms, no street-smart pimps, no corpses hung upside down, and no insane doctors. The dream was over. This was reality.

"Thanks, *barmaid*," I said smiling.

"No problem, *squire*," Kim said and winked.

About the Author

Bill Jacques is a seasoned writer, having published numerous short stories, poems, and articles in various small press publications over the years. He is also heavily involved with the New England film industry, having appeared in over twenty films, two television shows, commercials and two music videos. He has written, acted in and directed several independent films in the past two years. Bill is currently a Special Needs teacher in Hingham, Massachusetts and holds a Master's Degree in Special Education. He also serves on his town's Finance Committee.

Bill and his wife Cheryl are the very proud parents of their two sons, Nolan and Joshua. Both boys are also involved with music and film. Bill's love of children extends to the many coaching experiences he has been involved with in his home town of East Bridgewater, Mass.

Bill is currently promoting his most recent unpublished suspense novel, *Unsound Reflections*. He is also in preproduction of his full length feature film entitled, *The Test*.

Order Books for Your Friends!

Or other books from Sweet Dreams Publishing of Massachusetts!

Simply Visit us at:

www.PublishAtSweetDreams.com
and click on the book title to order online.

OR: Fill out the form below and mail your order to:

Sweet Dreams Publishing of MA
5 Federal Street
Weymouth, MA 02188
Attn: Lisa Akoury-Ross

Title: (check which title or both)
- ❏ A Wayward Oath: $10.95 Quantity: _____
- ❏ New American Cuisine for Today's Family: $15.00 Quantity: _____

Total Number of books: _____ Subtotal: _____

Shipping: _____ $6.00

Total: _____

Name: _____

Street: _____

City, State, Zip: _____

Phone or email: _____

www.ingramcontent.com/pod-product-compliance
Lightning Source LLC
Chambersburg PA
CBHW030541180626
46810CB00005B/1957